# 1 Think before you post

REMEMBER THAT ONCE SOMETHING IS ONLINE, IT'S OFTEN THERE FOREVER.

# 2 Protect your personal information

AVOID SHARING IMPORTANT DETAILS LIKE PHONE NUMBERS AND ADDRESSES PRIVATE TO AVOID CYBERSTALKING OR IDENTITY THEFT.

# 3 Learn about privacy settings

UNDERSTAND HOW SOCIAL MEDIA PLATFORMS WORK SO YOU CAN CUSTOMIZE THEM ACCORDING TO YOUR PREFERENCES.

# 4 Be cautious when accepting friend requests

IMPORTANCE OF BEING CAUTIOUS WHEN ACCEPTING FRIEND REQUESTS

# 5 Say no to cyberbullying

SPEAK UP AGAINST BULLYING BEHAVIOR AND REPORT INCIDENTS TO ADULTS OR AUTHORITIES WHEN NECESSARY.

# 6 Enhance account security

ALWAYS USE STRONG PASSWORDS FOR BETTER PROTECTION OF ALL KINDS OF ONLINE ACCOUNTS

# 7 Identify scams and frauds online

RESEARCH RELEVANT TYPES OF SCAM MESSAGES SUCH AS PHISHING EMAILS/ADSIMS(ONLINE FRAUDULENT ADVERTISEMENT)

# 8 Oversharing should be avoided

ONLY SHARE THE PUBLIC INFO WHICH DOESN'T CONTRADICT WITH ANYONE

# 9 Always communicate in a polite manner

EVEN IF SOMEONE ELSE ISN'T RESPECTFUL TOWARDS YOUR VIEWS

# 10 Staying away from negative comments

IT'S GOOD NOT RESPONDING ON SOME HARSH/NEGATIVE/NONCONSTRUCTIVE STATEMENTS OR OPINIONS MADE OVER CONVERSATIONS

# THINK BEFORE YOU POST

This fun and engaging story teaches you the importance of being mindful of what you post on social media. Through a lively adventure with relatable characters, you will learn to think twice before sharing anything online.

Welcome to Social Media

# Think Twice Before You Post

In the land of social media, lived two best friends, Timmy and Sarah. They loved taking pictures and sharing them online. One day, they went on a road trip and took lots of exciting photos together. They were so excited to share them with their friends that they instantly posted all of them on social media.

The next day, they woke up to find that their pictures had gone viral and everyone was talking about them. At first, they were thrilled to see so many likes and comments. But soon, they noticed that not all the comments were kind or positive. Some people were making fun of their clothes, while others were criticizing their poses.

Timmy and Sarah felt embarrassed and hurt. They realized that they had not thought twice before posting and sharing everything with the world. They had not considered that not everyone on social media was friendly or well-intentioned.

Timmy and Sarah learned a valuable lesson that day. They understood that they needed to think twice before posting anything online. They decided to take down their photos and be more careful in the future. They also promised to be kind and respectful to others online, just like they would be in person.

And so Timmy and Sarah lived happily ever after, sharing their experiences with the world but always thinking twice before pressing the post button.

# PROTECT YOUR PERSONAL INFORMATION

This entertaining story teaches you the importance of protecting your personal information online. Through a whimsical tale featuring lovable characters and relatable situations, you will learn how to stay safe online and keep your private details away from prying eyes.

Hi Benny, This is Dan from first grade. What is your email address?

Dan is not on social media, don't message me.

# Guard Your Information Online

In the land of social media, there lived a friendly boy named Benny. Benny loved to use his computer and phone to chat with his friends, play games, and watch funny videos. One day, while Benny was scrolling through his feed, he received a message from a stranger claiming to be his long-lost cousin.

The stranger asked Benny for his home address, phone number, and email address. Benny thought it was exciting to have a new cousin, so he quickly shared all his information with the stranger. However, Benny quickly realized his mistake. The stranger started sending him lots of spammy emails, and Benny was not feeling well at all.

Benny learned an important lesson that day. He understood that he should never give out his personal information to anyone he did not know well or trust. He also learned how to keep his accounts and messages safe by using a strong password and two-factor authentication.

Benny decided to protect his personal information. He talked to his parents and elders, read safety tips online, and shared them with all his friends. He now knew the risks of sharing information online, and he was happy that he was safe again.

And so, Benny lived happily ever after, using his computer and phone to have fun while also guarding his personal information carefully.

# LEARN ABOUT PRIVACY SETTINGS

This engaging story follows a group of friends on an exciting adventure as they learn about online privacy settings. Through a fun and relatable tale, you will understand how privacy settings work and why they are essential for staying safe and comfortable online.

# The Treehouse Secret: An Adventure in Online Privacy

Today is the day of the big treehouse party! Emily, Jack, and Lily cannot wait to celebrate together in their cool secret hideout. They are all so excited to share the party pictures on social media that they quickly take dozens of photos!

But wait, something seems wrong. Jack notices a message from someone they do not know who seems to have seen everything happening in their treehouse! The friends immediately realized they had forgotten to check their privacy settings.

Panicking, Emily, Jack, and Lily rush to their computer and try to figure out how to set their privacy settings. They look at videos and read the instructions carefully, and finally, they find where to set their settings to private.

They suddenly feel much more comfortable and less exposed, knowing that their private moments and celebrations are safe from prying eyes. The friends feel relieved and safe, and they continue taking pictures and enjoying their party.

The friends learned an important lesson today. They understood that they could have fun and use social media safely by checking their privacy settings. They also knew that it was essential to keep their information private and not let strangers or unwanted people see their posts.

From that day on, the friends always made sure to check their privacy settings before posting anything online. They knew that this was the best way to protect their online identities and secrets. Emily, Jack, and Lily were happy knowing that they could still enjoy their treehouse parties while also staying safe and keeping their privacy intact!

# BE CAUTIOUS WHEN ACCEPTING FRIEND REQUESTS

This exciting story follows a young girl named Mia, who receives a mysterious friend request on social media. Through her journey to uncover the identity of the stranger, Mia learns about online safety and the importance of being cautious when accepting friend requests.

# The Mystery Friend Request

Mia loves using social media to connect with her friends and share pictures and stories. One day, while she was checking her newsfeed, she saw a stranger's friend request. The names looked familiar, but Mia could not remember who they were.

Without thinking twice, Mia accepted the request, and soon she started receiving many messages from strangers. He seemed friendly, but Mia had an uncomfortable feeling in her stomach. She decided to ask her older brother, who was very web-savvy, for advice.

Her brother told her that she should be cautious when accepting friend requests from strangers and that she should never share personal information with people she did not know. He also helped her understand that online identities could be faked and that people could pretend to be someone they are not.

Mia started to feel worried and nervous. Who was this stranger, and why did he want to be her friend? She decided to do some research and found out that the stranger had a fake profile and was not the friendly person he had pretended to be.

Mia learned a valuable lesson that day: She knew that she needed to be cautious when accepting friend requests and that she should always listen to her gut feeling. She also promised herself never to share any personal information online unless she was talking to someone trustworthy or official.

From that day on, Mia felt safer and more in control of her online identity. She knew that social media could be fun but also dangerous if not used with caution. Mia felt empowered and happy knowing that she was smarter and more alert about online safety!

# SAY NO TO CYBERBULLYING

This eye-opening story teaches you about the dangers of cyberbullying and how you can stand up to it. Through an exciting adventure with fun characters, you will learn to say no to cyberbullying and be kind online.

I hate it....

# The Cyberbully Adventure

In the world of social media, a group of friends, Colin, Ruby, and Jake, loved to share pictures and connect with their friends online. One day, they met a mean person online who started leaving rude comments on their posts. The group ignored the comments at first, but the bully would not stop, and soon it became a real problem.

The group did not know what to do, and they were scared to share with their parents or teachers. Then their cool Uncle Alex came to visit them and saw how unhappy they were. Their uncle taught them about cyberbullying and how they must take a strong stance against it.

The uncle told them that they could say no to the bully and report him to the concerned platform. They could also choose to block or unfollow the mean commenters. Finally, they could ask an adult to help them if they could not handle it alone.

The group felt relieved, and they started taking their uncle's advice. They reported the bully to the concerned platform and blocked him too. They also talked with their parents and teachers and understood that they had nothing to feel ashamed of, as cyberbullying is a frequent problem.

In the end, the group felt happier and safer. They knew that cyberbullying was not okay, and they had the power to stand up to it. They continued to use social media for fun and sharing but made sure to say no to cyberbullying and be kind to others online.

And so Colin, Ruby, and Jake lived happily ever after, enjoying their online adventures but always standing up to cyberbullying.

# ENHANCE ACCOUNT SECURITY

This exciting tale follows a young boy named Max, who learns about online safety and enhances his account security after his favorite video game account is hacked. Through an adventurous journey, Max discovers the importance of strong passwords and other security measures.

# The Secret Code to Online Safety

Max loved playing his favorite video game online and had worked hard to level up his character. One day, to his shock, he found out that his account had been hacked and all his progress had been erased!

Max felt upset and frustrated, but he decided to do something about it. He talked with his parents and learned about how to enhance his account security and protect his personal information.

Max learned that he needed to make strong passwords with a combination of letters, numbers, and symbols. He also learned that he could enable two-factor authentication, where he would have to enter a secret code after logging in to prove his identity.

Max felt confident now, and he changed all his account passwords to stronger ones. He also enabled two-factor authentication for all his accounts. He understood that these steps were necessary to protect his essential information and keep his accounts safe from hackers and cybercriminals.

Max felt proud of himself and was happy knowing that he was responsible and aware of online safety. He continued to play his favorite video game and explore social media with confidence and security.

And so Max got back to his online adventures feeling safer and more secure, with the secret code to online safety always in his pocket.

# IDENTIFY SCAMS AND FRAUDS ONLINE

This exciting story follows a young detective named Sarah, who solves a mystery surrounding social media fraud. Through her investigation, Sarah learns how to identify scams and frauds online and how to stay safe while browsing the internet.

# The Case of the Social Media Scam

Sarah loved solving mysteries and was excited to take on her latest challenge—a social media scam that was affecting many people in her town. Sarah heard that people were receiving messages from strangers claiming they had won a prize or lottery, but it was a scam to extract money or personal information.

Sarah decided to investigate and started researching scams and frauds. She found out that scams often appear as enticing offers or unbelievable opportunities but are, in fact, traps to collect personal information or money.

Sarah also learned that scammers could create fake profiles, pose as someone else, or use an identity that appears trustworthy. She knew that it was important to verify the source of the message or deal and not share any personal information without verifying the risks and benefits.

Sarah continued her investigation and uncovered a network of scammers who were operating from another city. She reported the culprits to the concerned authorities, who arrested them and stopped the scam from continuing.

Sarah realized that many people could fall for scams and frauds online, and it was essential to stay alert. She also learned that it was necessary to use strong passwords, update security software regularly, and educate others about online safety and security.

Sarah knew that she was now a responsible and knowledgeable internet user, capable of protecting herself and her community from online dangers.

And so, Sarah solved the case of the social media scam with her detective skills and online safety knowledge, always staying alert and aware of the risks and dangers that come with browsing the internet.

# OVERSHARING SHOULD BE AVOIDED

This heartwarming story follows a girl named Lily, who learns about the importance of not oversharing on social media. Through her adventure, Lily discovers that some secrets are meant to be kept private and learns how to be a responsible user of social media.

# The Social Media Secret-Keeper

Lily loved social media, and she liked to tell all her friends about her daily activities and experiences. She enjoyed posting pictures and sharing details about her life. Lily was especially excited when she received a friend request from someone she did not know but seemed friendly.

The stranger started chatting with her and asking her for her personal information, such as her phone number and address. Lily got caught up in the excitement and shared her information without realizing the potential risks. Soon after, Lily found out that the person was not who they claimed to be and started using her personal information to cause trouble.

Feeling upset and betrayed, Lily went to talk to her grandmother, who was wise and caring. She explained to Lily the possible dangers of oversharing on social media and how some secrets were meant to be kept private.

Her grandmother told her that while it was essential to express oneself freely, it was equally important not to share or reveal too much personal information online. She encouraged Lily to be responsible when using social media and to think before she shared anything online.

Lily learned a valuable lesson and understood that it was okay to keep some things private. She started using social media more strategically, posting only what was appropriate and not sharing too much. She was careful about her online friends and realized how important it was to prioritize cyber safety.

Lily felt empowered and happy, knowing that she was now using social media responsibly and looking out for her best interests. She continued to enjoy social media and share her experiences, but now with a newfound awareness of how to be a responsible user.

And so, Lily became the social media secret keeper, with the knowledge and wisdom to never share too much online and stay safe in the virtual world.

# ALWAYS COMMUNICATE IN A POLITE MANNER

This heartwarming story follows a boy named Alex who learns about the importance of communicating politely on social media. Through his friendship with a pen pal, Alex discovers how kind words can create meaningful and positive connections with others.

# The Polite Pen Pal

Alex loved writing and connecting with other people online. He had a pen pal named Mia who lived in a different country, and they loved sharing stories and ideas.

One day, Alex received a message from Mia that he did not like. It was not rude or offensive, but it was not polite either. Alex felt hurt and disappointed and did not know how to respond.

He talked to his wise grandmother, who told him that communicating politely and respectfully online was important. She taught him about the magic words like please, thank you, and sorry, and how they could make all the difference in positive interactions online.

Alex realized that his response to Mia should be polite and respectful, even though he did not like her message. He thanked her for her message and shared his thoughts politely and kindly.

To his surprise, Mia responded positively, and they had a meaningful conversation that created a stronger bond between them.

Alex learned that communicating politely and respectfully online could create meaningful and positive connections with others. He continued to use magic words in his online interactions, and he noticed that people respected him more.

Years later, Alex and Mia finally met each other in person, and they knew that their pen pal friendship was built on kindness, respect, and a love for writing.

And so, Alex the Polite Pen Pal showed that communicating politely online could create positive and meaningful connections with others, even across countries and cultures. He knew that with kindness and respect, he could make the world a better place, one message at a time.

# STAYING AWAY FROM NEGATIVE COMMENTS

This adventurous story follows a girl named Lily who learns about the importance of staying away from negative comments on social media. Through her outdoor journey, Lily discovers that by focusing on the positive, she can create a happier and healthier online life.

# The Happy Hiker

Lily was a happy and adventurous hiker who loved sharing her outdoor experiences online. She loved getting feedback and ideas from other hikers, but sometimes she encountered negative comments that made her sad and discouraged.

One day, while she was hiking, she ran into a friendly dog who led her to a wise old owl named Ollie. Ollie saw that Lily was sad and asked her what was wrong. Lily told Ollie about the negative comments she received online and how they made her feel.

Ollie suggested that Lily stay away from negative comments and instead focus on the positive. He told her that negative comments can be hurtful and that it is important to surround herself with positivity and kindness.

Lily was intrigued and asked Ollie for more advice. Ollie told her to share positive and inspiring stories, to connect with people who share her passions, and to focus on what makes her happy.

Lily tried Ollie's advice and started sharing positive stories and photos of her hikes. She connected with other hikers who shared her passion and inspired her to explore unfamiliar places.

The more she focused on the positive, the happier and more connected she felt. She realized that social media was just a tool, and how she used it was up to her.

One day, she received a negative comment on one of her posts, and she remembered Ollie's advice. She did not respond or engage with negativity, but instead stayed away and focused on the positive comments and feedback she received from her supportive followers.

Lily knew that Ollie's wise advice had worked, and she continued to share her outdoor experiences with joy and positivity.

And so, Lily the Happy Hiker became an ambassador of positivity online, inspiring others to stay away from negativity and to focus on the positive. She knew that with a little bit of positivity, she could create a happier and healthier online life.